FRAGMENTS
OF PLACE

FRAGMENTS
OF PLACE

AUDE

Translated from French by David Homel

Library and Archives Canada Cataloguing in Publication

Aude, 1947-
[Éclats de lieux. English]
Fragments of place / Aude ; translated from French by David Homel.

Short stories.
Translation of: Éclats de lieux.
Issued in print and electronic formats.
ISBN 978-1-55096-494-3 (paperback).--ISBN 978-1-55096-495-0 (epub).--
ISBN 978-1-55096-496-7 (mobi).--ISBN 978-1-55096-497-4 (pdf)

I. Homel, David translator II. Title. III. Title: Éclats de lieux. English.

PS8589.I77E4213 2016   C843'.54   C2015-906550-X
                                            C2015-906551-8

Design and Composition by Mishi Uroboros
Typeset in Janson Text and Trajan Pro fonts at Moons of Jupiter Studios

Published by Exile Editions Ltd ~ www.ExileEditions.com
144483 Southgate Road 14 – GD, Holstein, Ontario, N0G 2A0
Printed and Bound in Canada in 2015, by Marquis Books

We gratefully acknowledge, for their support toward our publishing
activities, the Canada Council for the Arts, the Government of Canada
through the Canada Book Fund, the Ontario Arts Council,
and the Ontario Media Development Corporation.

Canadian sales: The Canadian Manda Group, 664 Annette Street,
Toronto ON M6S 2C8 www.mandagroup.com 416 516 0911

North American and International Distribution, and U.S. Sales:
Independent Publishers Group, 814 North Franklin Street,
Chicago IL 60610   www.ipgbook.com   toll free: 1 800 888 4741

To all the women and men I have loved,
and they are numerous.

To all my readers, past, present, and future.

To all women and men of good will;
they are the majority on this planet.

Contents

A Foreword to My Readers | 1

The Spinners | 13

Taking Shelter | 18

Playing Knucklebones | 22

The Girls' Room | 23

The Jackals | 34

Exile | 38

Other People's Blood | 39

Indelible Virginia | 45

The Woman in the River | 51

The Wait | 56

A Living Soul | 60

Beyond Reproach | 65

A Drowning | 75

A Recurring Pattern | 76

Heart of Ice | 81

The Perfume of Ylang-Ylang | 83

Sapping | 90

The Woman in the Alley | 92

The Ultimate | 98

The Spinners (What Came Next) | 100

The goal is not to stay alive, but to stay human.
—GEORGE ORWELL, *1984*

The goal is not to build great temples on the outside, but to create temples of goodness and compassion on the inside, within our hearts.
—THE DALAI LAMA

A Foreword to my Readers:
Past, Present, and Future

All of it was written in a spirit of joy, in a time of catastrophe.
—Jean-Yves Leloup, *L'absurde et la grâce*

All books by all authors are written at a specific time in their lives, in their personal histories, and at a particular moment in the history of the world.

Sometimes it is difficult to detect what was happening in an author's life when she was writing the book, unless she – or he – gives us clues in the lines, or through interviews, or in some other way. In some cases, the date of publication will tell us about the historical period in which it was written.

Several of the stories in *Fragments of Place* were published long ago in literary magazines, especially in *XYZ: La revue de la nouvelle*.

Yet most were written over the course of the last five years, when great waves of violence and deep conflicts wracked the planet. In 2011, hope suddenly reappeared with the Arab Spring and other crucial events. Great social movements based on indignation have come forward around the world. In different ways and different contexts, they have called for improvements to the common good, for true democracy without violence and with justice for all citizens, including those of the future. The protection of our Earth, which has become urgent and vital, is of course part of these demands. Certainly today, before any future can be radiant, there is an enormous amount of work to do, complex and delicate and with the capacity to reconcile the many opposing forces, while extremely powerful economic, political, and religious factions try to maintain their domination and seize the upper hand and impose their vision.

Fragments of Place bears the mark of these pages of history.

This collection does not, however, reflect – except, perhaps, in one story – what I was going through in my personal life as I was writing. In my own small history, major upsets occurred that turned everything upside down.

༄

I was writing my most recent novel *Chrysalide*, published in 2006, when everything began to change. Yet in this novel, there are no echoes of my private upheaval.

For me, writing is the perfect way to travel through the vast and virtual expanse of my humanity, far beyond the limits of my identity. This turned out to be a saving grace in these circumstances, as it had been, previously, in others.

Seven years ago in June, I was informed that I had blood cancer; it was deadly and incurable. The prediction, including chemotherapy and stem-cell treatment, was two years at best.

Despite my death foretold, I decided to throw myself into the *Chrysalide* project that I had been intending to write before I received the fateful news. No matter what, that novel was inside me and I wanted to write it.

Writing is always very demanding, and it was even more so with my more than precarious health. But the book let me turn away from the world of sickness and death.

With the help of words, I built a character called Catherine ("Catou" for her intimates), a young woman of twenty-two, and then I slipped into her skin. I had to inhabit her fully, and blend into her and her reality. Catou, the narrator, is writing a sort of personal journal. I, Aude, couldn't write it for her, with my vocabulary, my style, and my experience. What a magnificent transmigration!

Afterward, my many encounters with students at the college level proved to me, beyond a doubt, that they considered Catou as one of them. I had succeeded my metempsychosis.

Thanks to the fabulous power of fiction, I could project myself into other experiences outside the ones typical of my age, sex, appearance, state of health, cultural belonging, and the choices I made through the course of my life. Through the writing and reading of fiction, my limits were wiped away and everything became possible.

After the diagnosis and prognosis, two years went by without the death foretold occurring. The treatments went on with their ups and downs. At times I came close to death, then recovered my strength.

꩜

Shortly after *Chrysalide* was published, despite my shaky health, I went back to writing, short stories this time. Little by little, the idea of a collection began to take shape. Writing isolated stories is one thing, but to see a collection come together is completely different.

I applied for a grant from the Canada Council for the Arts, unsure whether I could actually complete the project. I received what I asked for, and I must admit that the acceptance was a very strong stimulant that helped me with my writing despite extremely difficult times. I thank the Canada Council for the Arts for its support; up until now, it might not have been able to gauge its importance to me.

A year later, when I had written further stories, I sent the results to Gaëtan Lévesque, my publisher, along with the "Detailed Description of My Project" that I had submitted to the Canada Council. Gaëtan was my constant companion as I made my way. He acted without ever exerting pressure, always urging me to look after myself first. Every time I sent him a new story, he read it immediately. And every time he responded, and what he wrote gave me wings to fly. I can never thank him enough for believing in my writing all through the years, and for backing up his trust with concrete actions, over and over. From *The Indiscernible Movement* in 1997 to *Fragments of Place* in 2012, his support has been unwavering.

Of course I couldn't always write at a pace I would have liked to maintain. But the fascination, exaltation, and happiness that arose from immersing myself in words and characters were awaiting me each time.

Was I able to carry out my project completely? Not entirely, even if *Fragments of Place* is now a book, and has everything necessary to form an honest collection of stories.

Inside me, I still have other stories asking to be born. I can clearly see characters and scenes. I hear sentences in my head. There are pathways to explore, words to follow up on.

But I'm afraid that time and energy are deserting me...

If that's not the case, if death continues to circle without urging me onto the dance floor, I intend to write the stories turning inside me, the ones I have not had time to attend to. I might publish them in that wonderful, stimulating magazine called *XYZ: La revue de la nouvelle*, also edited by Gaëtan Lévesque.

Sometimes, when I feel defiant, cocky, and in the mood to laugh, I raise my middle finger to the sky and, once again, at the end of a new story, I shout, "Fuck death!"

Can death grab me by the hide if I'm not inside it anymore? Can it catch up to me if I am camouflaged within the skin of my characters? Death doesn't know how to read – everyone knows that. It's too busy scouring the countryside.

Actually, I'm not at war with death. I am toying with it, as it toys with me. It started first! But I have learned to live with it. It is part of my life. And who knows, maybe one day I'll be the one to lead it onto the dance floor.

To give you a better idea of everything that was bubbling away inside me, and continues to simmer, regarding *Fragments of Place*, I'll let you read the "Detailed Description" that I submitted to the Canada Council as part of my grant application.

DETAILED DESCRIPTION OF THE PROJECT.

Currently I have five short stories that, though all very different, are related at a deeper level, which makes me feel I have a true collection in gestation, and not just disparate stories.

One of them, "The Spinners," would be the first in the collection, since it sets down what the issues will be in the rest of the book. In this story, the Fates, who spin and spool off, then cut the thread of human life, have decided to stop giving the gift of life to humans:

Outside, the madness of men, already so great, had gone beyond all limits in its fanaticism, cupidity, barbarity, and indifference. Nothing could appease their greedy gaze.

When other women came to ask asylum and protection from them, the three sisters decided to stop spinning the silky thread of life that was their gift to men. They ceased spooling it across fields of time, then cutting it off, when the hour was right, to preserve the world's harmony. It just wasn't worth the trouble anymore.

This story is different from the others that will follow (the four that have been written and those to come) because it gives a complete picture, a view "from above," a superior point of view on what is happening "down below." The fate of human beings is in the hands of these three women.

The other stories in the collection will carry us into the field, down below, here in our world made of chaos, and we will experience the intimate lives being lived in different places on the planet. There will be war, social instability, and totalitarianism. Other places live in peace, and seem to be harmonious and secure, but even there, life implodes more each day, undermined by silent, destructive violence.

One of the stories I have written, "The Jackals," takes place in a tent in a refugee camp. Four women are hiding there. Two Jackals are on the prowl, waiting for the armed guards to leave, as they have come to escort another woman refugee; when the coast is clear, the Jackals will attack. "The Jackals" is the name I chose for a group of male refugees who have taken over the camp and are terrorizing the inhabitants.

The Jackals are on the lookout, prowling in silence, in groups of two or three, near the tents where death has left its seal and made room for others.

Lilia heard two of them walking close by, so close they brushed against the canvas. They even urinated on it.

The very short story "Playing Knucklebones" could be set in our world, in our peaceful and "civilized" universe, where survival is not a way of life.

The title of the collection came to me after I read the five stories in a row. *Fragments of Place*. Through its multiple meanings, it creates a strong generating principle for the stories to come.

Fragments can refer to horrible things, as in the story "Taking Shelter," in which two famous war photographers are now trapped, after a career of successfully capturing moments of astonishment and horror. They spent their lives hoping to faithfully bear witness, through their photos, to the dreadful events in countries that most people prefer to forget. But now they are chasing after horror the way others crave a drug they can't live without.

Sometimes, in situations of extreme tension, they secretly wished that the worst would befall them, right before their eyes. That a rocket would shred human flesh, that the carnage would begin, that heads and hands would be torn away, right now, in front of them, as they trained their telescopic lenses on possible targets.

Fragments of a pulverized world, beyond what is imaginable or possible, "a common grave where bodies are ground into the rocky soil with a bulldozer, in order to obliterate all traces of the massacre," "a wall splattered with death."

But also, *fragments* of different places, inner worlds destroyed in various ways by other human beings. Fragments of families, couples, mistreated children, stripped of their childhood.

Fragments of dreams.

Fragments of bodies falling apart in illness, bones growing fragile, breasts assaulted by the scalpel, limbs amputated, no longer responding to messages sent by the brain.

Fragments of memory adrift, having lost everything that was stored, what we thought was our lives, but has now run aground like in a shipwreck.

Fragments of everything that disappears as age carries out its slow and pitiless work on body and mind, as it mocks everything that once was important, laying low love, parents, and the dearest friends.

In *Fragments of Place*, there is also the possibility of dismissing fear, taboos, rules, censorship, cages, and ordinary ways of seeing, thinking, and living, so that freedom, desire, light, and hope shine through. And with it solidarity, so precious and necessary.

Bursts of laughter; outbursts of joy. Children's voices in the street. Sunbursts.

Here, as elsewhere. Inside and out.

༈

This project was so fertile that it is hard to staunch the flow of creation it continues bringing forth.

FRAGMENTS
OF PLACE

THE SPINNERS

In the beginning, they were three.

Three sisters come from the night.

For an eternity, they had spun time between their fingers, beautiful and silent, their bodies and minds dedicated to men, in the spacious room where sunlight and fresh air freely entered through veils undulating in the breeze.

Their dresses of raw silk whispered sweetly with each of their movements, like the wings of a dragonfly.

The days slipped by, easily, governed by the cycle of life. The primal forces were still in control, and no one thought to question everything at all times.

But they aren't alone anymore now, in the vast dwelling where voices and footfalls are muted, as if someone were dying in the next room.

Some time ago, nine other women came seeking refuge with them. When the nine arrived, they were in terrible condition. Outside, they had been tracked down, beaten, and raped.

The three sisters were in consternation, and took them in and cared for them, setting aside their work, neglecting the patient and secretive woman's work that creates life and accompanies it to the end.

The wool with its rich and varied colours, the wooden frame, the distaff, and the scissors – all were cast aside, into forgetfulness.

Even in the worst moments, and there had been many, had they thought they would reach such an extreme decision.

Now there were twelve of them.

Most of the women were at the dazzling yet fragile crest of maturity, just before everything begins to turn, slowly but inexorably, to drag them silently toward oblivion, covering them with a fine layer of chalk under which their features will grow indistinguishable, their eyes sightless, until they disappear entirely. But that will not happen to these women. They are of another lineage.

Moira, one of the three sisters, was the eldest among them. She alone was dressed in black. She was the most fearsome of them. She stood straight, majestic, and inflexible.

The youngest of the refugees wasn't even twenty. She had the graceful movements of a doe. Sometimes she could scarcely contain the wild energy that sent her bounding toward the outside despite the dangers and despite the fear that had entered her like a poison.

Now they were living by lamplight, even during the day. The windows had been blocked by heavy draperies that let nothing in from outside.

They spoke very little, and when they did, they murmured.

They poured each other tea in delicate porcelain cups. Or fine liqueurs in crystal goblets. They drank with the smallest of sips.

Some began to hum songs, recite poetry, and play the flute. Others took a step or two, as if to dance. Then embraced one another, but it did not last. Suddenly they stopped, fell silent, and froze in their tracks, uncertain what to do next.

One of them would free the long braids of another, then unhurriedly comb her hair out, then braid it again, decorating it again with tiny stars.

Their hands slipped nonchalantly over the rounded surfaces of the vases, along the mahogany tables, the embroidery of the armchairs, the fabric of the dresses. Sometimes they caressed a face or a shoulder.

They put on makeup. They arranged their hair. They dressed. They prepared for festivities that would never come.

And they knew it.

They removed their makeup. Rinsed their faces with rose water, took baths in sweet-smelling oil. Put their makeup back on again. Applied polish to their faultless nails.

A single perfume of lily of the valley, ferns, and Spanish moss, like a magnetic fluid, brought their bodies together.

The women tried to be calm even if, inside, they felt completely lost. They supported each other to avoid despair.

They were what must never die, what must be preserved if life is to continue.

Outside, the madness of men, already so great, had gone beyond all limits in its fanaticism, cupidity, barbarity, and indifference. Nothing could appease their greedy gaze.

When the other women came to ask asylum and protection from them, the three sisters decided to stop spinning the silky thread of life that was their gift to men. They ceased spooling it across fields of time, then cutting it off, when the hour was right, to preserve the world's harmony. It just wasn't worth the trouble anymore.

Since that day, on the outside, the cradles have been desperately empty.

Despite that obvious sign, men continued to strike out blindly and tear each other apart in time that had ceased to exist, that generated nothing but terror endlessly sowed, everywhere, nothing but a growing sense of greed, and misfortune never before seen.

Death, until that day, did not appear to deliver those who could not stand being sick and old anymore. Nor those who could not brook this world of pains. Now, no one died anymore, and neither was anyone born. Men had entered the eternity they had always wished for, but that turned out to be hellish. The hell they had created.

In the spacious room, the youngest of the women came to sit at the feet of the oldest. She was crying.

In a lengthy plea, she asked for grace for men who, outside, had forgotten how precious the fleeting and precarious measure of life was, the length they had been granted.

She wanted to return with the others to that universe, though they had been harried out of it with violence. For she knew that, down below, the majority of humans tried to resist the best they could the madness of the all-powerful, pitiless minority. They needed the women to believe that their resistance was not in vain.

But for that to be, the three sisters would have to take up their work again.

The time had not come, and may never come again.

TAKING SHELTER

They were waiting for the night, or the rain, in this country where it never rains, where the desert stretches on forever, deadly in its sameness.

They wanted to emerge from the narrow, burning shadow where they had sought refuge. To escape. Leave behind this hell and return to their reassuring place of origin where you can breathe the air and walk out in the open without fearing flash desiccation or massacre.

The sand and the scorching air were burning them alive. Their dehydrated eyelids scraped against their dry eyes every time they blinked. It was too painful to keep their eyes closed.

The two men hardly moved at all, crouching under what remained of their desert vehicle, dragging themselves out of the sun's rays that tracked them down, slowly, turning endlessly around the metal carcass, trying to slip underneath it and reach them with its fiery tongue and incinerate them alive, with all the patience in the world.

They waited for the night, but it had stopped gracing them with its visit some time ago. The sun no longer went down, obsessed with the men it was hunting pitilessly, wanting to strip the flesh off their bones and turn them into fossils, for remembrance.

These photographers had come here to be faithful witnesses to the dreadful events in this country that others preferred to forget.

They had been doing this for years now. At the beginning, they had believed in their work. They returned devastated from their travels, traumatized by the images they had brought back.

They believed in what they were doing, but with time, something had changed. It wasn't visible, but they felt it. They never spoke about it together, or with anyone else, but they were stricken with the same malaise and they knew it. The more horrible and unspeakable the scene, the more excited they felt, indecently, like an ever-growing greed for horror, because its effect had dulled over time and they needed ever stronger doses.

Sometimes, in situations of extreme tension, they secretly wished the worst would happen. That a rocket would shred human flesh, that the carnage would begin, that heads and hands would be torn away, right now, in front of them, as they trained their telescopic lenses on possible targets.

Fortunately, several times they were lucky enough to be at the exact spot and exact time to capture the unspeakable. In front of a child bursting into fragments in full sunlight as he stepped on a mine. Or that other person they didn't even see in the images, buried under tons of rubble deep in a tin mine; they saw only the mother digging through the ruins with her bloody hands, her mouth open with screams you could not hear. Thick, ashen dust covered her face that had become a stiff mask where only her eyes burned like glowing coals.

These were legendary photographs like others they had taken, and had travelled the world.

I, too, stared at those photos with real emotion, in that magazine I often bought despite the high price, because I wanted to be well informed, I wanted to look reality in the eye, its raw truth as I sat comfortably in my leather armchair among the flowers, a glass of aged port by my side.

I was so absorbed in the profound reflections those images awoke in me that at first I did not notice that evening was taking its time to settle, and strangely so: the daylight was lingering in undue fashion.

Little by little, people stepped out into the street, amazed by the presence of the light and the sun's unusual warmth at this late hour in the season.

I went out and joined those people.

Then amazement gave way progressively to concern, then fear, then terror as we faced the pitiless violence of the sun.

We fled the daylight and sought shelter in endless artificial night. We put on sophisticated survival suits. We barricaded ourselves in inviolable safe rooms.

We would not be touched.

And we will stay there, secure, behind our armour, prisoners of our shelters, our hearts completely desiccated.

PLAYING KNUCKLEBONES

Hidden under a pile of thick blankets, François, ten years old.

It's three o'clock.

His father was yelling again. And hitting him.

"I'll break that nasty streak of yours, I swear I will!"

With a nutcracker, one by one, François broke the knuckles of his right hand.

THE GIRLS' ROOM

Through her memory, the woman kept the room inside a hermetic bubble. It was a sacred territory defended tooth and nail by powerful spells, ingenious constructions of down from blue chicks, marbles, cat mustaches, fairy tales, and barley sugar drops.

But a few years ago, that idyllic image had failed. Too many cracks brought down the fragile structure.

Deep down, she knew that one day, without anything being visible from outside, the girls' sacred room had been devastated forever.

Neither she nor her sister managed to discover what had caused such disaster. They remembered nothing, except that everything had changed, and that afterward, the damage could not be repaired.

They researched, and they asked questions. The documents they found explained nothing, but did confirm that something very serious had occurred. The people who might have had something to say preferred silence. Later, they disappeared.

The current owners of the old residence where the woman once lived had remodelled and repainted the ceiling with its flowers made of plaster, and repaired the room's crumbling walls. They shored up and sanded the floor. They stripped the paint off the woodwork and replaced the old sashes.

But the cracks in the plaster quickly reappeared. At the angles, the wooden window frame broke into constellations of fine mould that was a downy rose colour, and the floorboards pulled away from one another all over again. Here and there, you could look down onto an underground world.

After their vain attempts to combat the resurgence of the past, the occupants decided to domesticate the hidden part of their dwelling. Instead of turning it into the guest room as they had intended, they set up their bookcases there, and their reading chairs, and a few paintings they particularly liked.

They got more and more attached to the house where past lives had taken hold over time, in the wood floors worn down in certain spots by the steps of everyone who had, as they had, walked back and forth, over and over again, without end. As if a large part of a life's secrets could be found in this ordinary, intimate coming and going, a few familiar people in an enclosed space, for they continued to walk there long after they had departed from this place.

The two men saw stories everywhere in filigree form, like a rich high-warp tapestry, outmoded now, the image faded to the point of being unreadable, where, in a succession of tableaux, the life that once flourished between these walls, and death as well, was recounted.

The woman had no trouble distinguishing certain patterns, here and there.

Like the paper with the long-leaf motif, on the walls of the long hallway, pasted there by the mother and the grandmother with a wide brush dipped in flour glue that they had vigourously stirred on the stove the evening before.

Or the fake fireplace in the living room and the mother sitting by the window, late in the evening, waiting for the man to return. Sometimes the girl would wake up and come and count cars with her mother so she would stop crying.

Maybe there was crying in the girls' room as well, and the younger one didn't know it. Maybe she should have stayed there, with her sister. But who can tell now?

The woman pictured the girls' faces pressed against the screen door, at the back of the large kitchen, as twilight fell. They were watching the alley, sensitive to the slightest sound.

During the day, the alley was their playground. They turned into princesses along with their girlfriends who came out to play with them, running through the yards where spiral stairs alighted and clotheslines hung. When the sun lowered, their mothers appeared on the back balconies and called their names into thin air. The girls dropped their games and went home without dragging their feet. When evening fell, the alley belonged to the Ogre.

Once they were inside, they stood quietly behind the screen, listening for the squeaky old rickety carriage of the Child Stealer. He went by every evening. If he caught a child, he would stuff her in the back of his carriage, and tape her mouth, then carry her off to someplace unknown.

Some girls had seen it happen. But they couldn't describe it; their lips were sealed.

Everything from that lost world returned pell-mell in the woman's memory. Fragile glass bubbles that held a living fragment of the past issued from her mouth. They rose into the air and floated there, then burst with a sound like tinsel.

She could still hear the reassuring tic-tic-tic of the sewing machine in the kitchen. She felt the smell and the crackling of the laundry stiffened by the cold when it was brought inside. And the irregular beating of her mother's heart as she tried to lull her youngest to sleep in the big rocking chair.

The woman gave her memories to the two men without caring to make a coherent, finished story. The story was full of holes and hermetic chambers.

She would never find the missing or hidden pieces. She knew as much. When she left here, her quest would end. Once and for all, she would give up on finding what, one day, had destroyed the little girls' room.

The men followed her through the house, quiet, and attentive.

Thanks to the woman, they could reach down to one of the strata of this place, and add their own chapter to it. Their cries of love, of pain, of anger, their periods of silence, their happiness, and the difficulty they had living together, those things added a layer and joined what everyone who had preceded them here had experienced. How many times had they lain down in beds like theirs in the big room and made meals, every day, as they did, in the same kitchen, no matter how much the décor had changed?

They knew that death slipped into this house, the way it had many times before. They heard its discreet footsteps in the night, patient and polite, awaiting the youngest of the two men it would soon claim.

The woman stood in the middle of the room where the two men liked to sit and talk, and enter the stories locked in the books around them, that had seemingly nothing to do with them, but in which they discovered themselves all the same.

She turned her eyes in their direction as if to make sure they were still there, with her, in the present, so she would not slip between the floorboards.

Before she rang the doorbell, the woman reached into her bag and took out the photo of the two girls sitting on the front steps. The big copper doorknob that she and her sister liked to shine to a polish was still there.

The man who opened the door listened to the woman, then took the photo she held out. The second man, clearly weakened with sickness, appeared and both examined the picture of the two little sisters, three and four years old, sitting very close together, the younger one's head leaning on the older one's shoulder.

The photo had been taken back when the little girls' room was an enchanted world away from everyone.

Even if the arrival of the youngest had not been easy.

She was born quickly and almost without pain. Everyone was amazed, as if the baby was in a hurry to see the light of day.

Not long after she came home in her mother's arms, she began to cry, and never stopped, or so it seemed, for weeks on end.

She was hungry. No one knew that. She was starving. Her need was so strong she could not learn how to suckle. Each time, she flew into a rage and her feverish, useless agitation exhausted her.

Late in the evening, after her mother had tried one last time to give her the breast, after she had set her in the cozy crib, then taken her again and rocked her a while more, humming her another song, the fateful moment would arrive when her mother, beyond fatigue, would disappear, she, too in tears.

On those evenings, the little girl's frenetic cries lost the power to draw her mother to her side.

And after an eternity, the child's strident cries grew weaker and slowly turned into a sound like a puppy's futile whimpering.

Then, there was silence.

In the other rooms of the house, people breathed easier. The kid had finally fallen asleep.

But nothing was further from the truth. Her eyes were wide open. Her body had turned to stone. She stopped moving, and hardly breathed at all, petrified by emptiness.

One night, like all the others when the little girl seemed to be dead, something magical happened. The girl felt a luminous presence in the sinister room. There was another little girl there, not much bigger than she was.

From that moment on, her nights and her days were illuminated. The other girl made her terrible thirst tolerable.

Then there were two.

Some time later, the real problem of the child's hunger was resolved. The child and the mother stopped crying and everything went back to normal.

The girls' room was an enchanted place for another few years. But little by little, toxic air began to saturate the atmosphere in the rest of the dwelling.

Then, without the girls knowing how or why, thick smoke filled their room and everything went black.

The room seemed the same, but the younger girl had lost her way. Everything looked the way it was before, but that was just a trap, a snare that would catch her limbs and bring her down.

Her big sister was there, but entirely absorbed in fighting, with desperate energy, an invisible but pitiless predator. As if something or someone was slowly bleeding her of her substance, surreptitiously sucking away her life.

The big sister who had once been all light was slowly darkening, but without dying, though locked in a block of silence.

Beneath her pretty cotton embroidered dresses with the bees'-nest pattern, she was burning alive. Her body twisted with pain and she fell in convulsions to the floor. Her mouth was deformed by screams, but no one heard, or wanted to hear.

She had to be calmed. Her lips sewn shut. Her memory burned clear. Made inoperative.

This was done, without explanation, with the help of powerful drugs.

The games were over. The dolls, massacred.

Nothing had ever happened. Everything was fine.

And that was the tragedy.

The youngest spent her days and nights looking in vain for her big sister in the ruins of their room. But she had disappeared.

In the house, the denial concerning her disappearance was so complete that it seemed as though the younger girl had invented everything. Not just her sister's absence, but her very presence in the first place – everything.

Her sister was replaced by a clone that looked so much like her you would be hard pressed to tell them apart. But the exact replica did not speak, did not laugh, did not sing. She knew nothing of their sibylline language, their secret alliance, and the way they shared everything.

For a time, the room became an optical illusion that made the younger girl doubt all that she saw, including her own existence.

Everything looked normal for the others. No one seemed to have noticed the misfortune that had befallen the dwelling. She alone sought what was lost, her luminous big sister who, when she arrived, so they said, a red carpet had been unrolled from the door to the street in the middle of winter, and all flags were made to fly.

Then, one day, the little girl understood that a baby was growing in her mother's stomach.

When that child entered the house, there were no celebrations to mark his arrival.

The little boy did not have a room. There was no room in the house for the newborn.

From the start, the girl was afraid for him.

She slipped talismans into his diapers to save him from the evil forces she felt prowling all around him. If she could have, she wouldn't have let anyone near him to keep something or someone from doing him harm, the way they had done to her sister.

She feared that her little brother would also disappear in inexplicable fashion. Small children were so easily lost in this sinister place.

But he didn't disappear. His mother did.

One morning, very early, she left as a siren screamed out its misfortune.

The child saw her again, several days later. The body displayed on white satin was cold, stiff, and silent. The little girl called and called, but there was no more mother inside.

The entire house sank along with the mother, then disappeared into a vast black hole.

Just like that, the little girls, each in her own direction, were thrown into the dormitories of death.

A few wane nightlights placed high on the walls made the place look like the catacombs. Bedside tables separated thirty or so narrow beds.

Under the ecru blankets and the scratchy sheets were pale, unmoving children who, like them, seemed to be sleeping. But none of the little girls was asleep. They were dead.

Yet in the morning, each bravely assumed her assembly-line life, without anyone realizing they had disappeared.

When evening came again, they died all over again, in silence. Again and again. Night after night.

Suddenly the woman remembered where she was. She was standing in the middle of the present.

The big sister and the little brother had died, for real, several years ago.

Before they disappeared forever, the woman was able to find them again.

Today, that's the only thing that counts.

As the woman looks on, the past slips into the confusion between the ill-fitting floorboards.

THE JACKALS

There was still an hour to go before curfew, but Lilia was huddling in her tent with the three other women with whom she shared her shelter. They had closed the canvas flap that served as a door. The heat was unbearable, but less threatening than the dangers from without.

Tasmine, the oldest, was lying on a mat. She hadn't stirred for several days. Soraya was attending to her. She was whispering prayers in her ear, moistening her lips with drops of water, keeping away the flies from her eyes and mouth, and bathing her forehead.

Soraya and Tasmine came to the camp ten months ago. They were among the survivors of an exodus during which more than half of those who had tried to escape the attack were killed. Among the dead were Soraya's children.

Aïcha was sleeping in Lilia's arms. Fever had blotted out the anxiety that twisted her stomach into a knot. She was eight years old. Her memory was already filled to the brim. They met during the thirty-eight-day march that led them, with the others, to this camp. They had become inseparable ever since the night when, under an indigo sky sewn with stars, as beautiful as a picture book, Aïcha was raped for the first time.

Lilia looked at her pen. When fear came over her, as it was doing now, she kept it in her hand.

Waterproof. An unnecessary guarantee. It hadn't rained for more than two months. And the refugees didn't receive the promised daily ration of water to drink, cook the rice in, and wash, a ration determined and written down somewhere, far away, in some official document, in a place where water ran freely. Here, people stood in line every four days, sometimes for hours under a burning sun, to get just enough of it, and just enough food not to starve to death. Some died anyway, every day, from lack of food and everything else.

Fade proof. The ink from this pen was guaranteed highest quality. Lilia thought she would enjoy this guarantee for many years in the future. When you're twenty-four, that's normal.

Lilia came from an urban background more educated and Westernized than the others. Some traditions were still respected, but many had fallen to the wayside because they were obsolete, unjust, and inhuman, even for the men.

There was no more ink in the transparent cylinder of her pen. Before, she would have thrown it away and replaced it with a new one. But now she held onto it like a precious object. Here, you didn't throw anything away. You always found new uses for the few objects you could keep.

A thin metal point held in your hand a few centimetres from someone's eye – that might make for a powerful dissuasive argument. But not all the time.

Lilia hadn't let go of the pen since those hundred or so new refugees showed up a few hours ago. They were still beneath the big canvas shelter by the guard post near the main entrance. But very soon, they would be escorted through the labyrinth of the camp toward the tents to which they were assigned, ones in which someone had just died, or would die soon.

Tasmine was breathing her last.

Lilia wasn't afraid of the new arrivals, most of them women, completely exhausted, stunned by the horror they had witnessed, and had suffered, wanting only one thing, to collapse and sleep, and reach complete amnesia as quickly as possible.

Lilia closed her hand over her pen.

The Jackals were on the lookout, prowling in silence, in groups of two or three, near the tents where death had left its seal and made room for others.

Lilia heard two of them walking close by, so close they brushed the canvas. They even urinated on it.

In every tent, from the lips of every man and woman rose a single desperate prayer to a God who could not hear them since he had stopped existing.

The new arrivals, divided in groups according to different sectors, were escorted to their respective tents by armed guards. The latter would disappear once their job was done.

Then the spoils could be divided up.

The Jackals would burst into the tents, strip the new arrivals of the little they had saved, rape the women, and brutally beat the men to show them who the masters were here.

Then they would go on their way, talking and laughing heartily, and return to their quarters where no one dared venture, not even the armed guards, despite the fact that they were refugees, too.

The two Jackals stopped. They took up position by the opening to the tent, their legs spread, their arms crossed, their eyes as cutting as a blade. Any moment now, the guards were going to push someone inside.

Lilia and Soraya had hidden little Aïcha underneath the mat where Tasmine lay. Their bodies would offer protection.

EXILE

Everything is black. India ink. More opaque than a starless night deep in the woods. Not the slightest ray of light under the door. No glow between the blinds, no nightlight.

Thick tar crept across the floor of the room and began to climb. Slowly, it covered everything: the walls, the furniture, everyone.

Even his body disappeared. The man couldn't see his feet or hands. Nothing. He couldn't move to make sure he was still there. Yet he didn't feel he was elsewhere.

The silence was complete.

He had stopped hearing Hildegard of Bingen singing through what seemed like cotton battien. And the muffled slipping of footsteps and the rustling of rich fabric. He'd stopped sensing the low voices of the people who, for hours, had attended to him, stroking his face and head.

All sound had been consumed, down to the lowest murmur.

OTHER PEOPLE'S BLOOD

My legs suddenly stopped moving and my body, halted in its forward motion, wavered a moment, then recovered its balance so I would not have to put my foot on the linoleum of the Department of Hematology and Oncology.

The floor of this imposing corridor was so shiny it looked like water.

Yesterday, on the way out, I noticed that the cleaning staff had brought in heavy equipment used to wash, strip, and wax the linoleum. I didn't pay much more attention. The work would be done through the evening and the night.

I continued walking and headed for reception, where I checked in for a transfusion. Then I dropped the documents providing the necessary information into the pigeonhole by the door of Treatment Room B.

As I waited for the invitation into that room, my eyes returned to the freshly waxed half of the long corridor.

They had created a shallow pool, carefully designed to reflect the surroundings. A mirror of water. I leaned over. The mirror was so faithful I could see myself clearly.

In it I also discovered the reflection of the many closed doors that lined either side, heavy with the drama that took place behind them, the images of wheelchairs in duplicate, the solid handrails that ran close to the floor, and the large posters on the walls that described, upside down and cast onto the floor, the intolerable illnesses that those who venture here are afflicted with.

I felt trapped in this heavy universe, grown heavier still by its duplication.

I decided to go into the section of the corridor with a duller finish where the transformation would take place tomorrow night.

But it was no better. On this side, the linoleum was splattered with stains of every variety. Millions of germs must have been proliferating there and spreading out in all directions.

I left the contamination zone and returned to the mirror in which sickness and death dwelled and evolved before my eyes.

The reflecting pool of the Taj Mahal displays a tomb. Yet nothing is macabre there. On the surface of the water is reflected, in inverted form, the sublime mausoleum that transcends death, magnifies love, and glorifies life. In the mirror of water, many things are visible: the cypresses that border it, the birds, and the sky above that turns the immutable white marble tomb into a living soul, moving and alive, changing colour and mood.

In the water of the hematology-oncology corridor, life was teeming there, too.

It was a place of encounters. Discreet glances, soft smiles, and understanding nods. Sometimes a few words were exchanged. Though we didn't know each other, we were comrades. I knew nothing of the exact circumstances that brought the other people to this place, and they knew nothing of mine, but we understood all the same. And that was enough to inspire a kind of tenderness that imposed no conditions, no confessions, and no expectations.

Finally they called me. I entered the arena of extreme combat.

The enemy was invisible yet ubiquitous, which made it terrifying. Its weapons were all the more terrible, since we hardly understood them at all. It manoeuvred in the secrecy of our cells, making them veer madly off course. They forgot everything about their position and their vital role. They started multiplying and invading us.

Yet our bodies were not completely defenceless. Fearless warriors held constant vigil. Most of the time, we knew nothing of their struggles against chaos. Their victories happened on a daily basis, and they were numerous, though discreet and won in silence.

In the room, we could hear the *beep-beep* of the transfusion pumps that shot atomic charges into our bloodstream to exterminate the part of us that was killing us. Many healthy cells were destroyed in the process, collateral damage, inevitable in wartime.

In this place, unspeakable things happened behind banal appearances. You just had to settle into an armchair for a while, or on a stretcher, to see that.

We were not passive spectators who entered the chemo-therapy room to observe what occurred in this place of taboos.

We were more involved than the ethnologist who went to live among some exotic, distant tribe. Even if that person tried to be one with the life of the tribe, and tried for years, he would always remain on the outside.

Whereas we who were lying here, our hands pierced by needles, were undergoing mutation. Just a word, only one, and we were catapulted into the ranks of the Stricken. Never again would we be part of the Intact. Even if we displayed the appearance of a cure.

There were seven of us here, plus eight more in an adjoining room linked by a narrow corridor that had been turned into a small command post.

Today, no chemo for me. The most recent treatment had been an ordeal for my red blood cells.

I chose an armchair instead of a stretcher. I felt less diseased that way. Sometimes all it takes is something small to make me feel less sick, or not sick at all. An article of clothing. A look. Desire that rises like sap.

A nurse came up to me.

The first time I entered this room, I thought the atmosphere would be saturated with sadness and discour-agement, and that an almost mortuary gravity would be the order of the day. That's because I didn't know about these women coming and going from patient to patient, dispensing care with disconcerting ease. They talked and laughed, both concentrated and light-hearted. On that first day I understood that, thanks to them, this place had nothing morbid about it. On the contrary: here, life was celebrated.

As months went by, or years in some cases, a bond grew between these women and us. A respectful familiarity that gave us a name, and them, too.

The nurse, Christine, inserted a needle into my left hand. An IV drip would gently widen my vein and prepare me for the great Encounter.

The most intimate kind of encounter: a disturbing connection between myself and someone I didn't know would soon take place.

That other person would slowly penetrate me and impregnate me with that unctuous red substance that flowed through every part of his body, driven by his heart.

He would give me the ruby-red blood that ran through his veins.

During this long, intense encounter, I would not see his face, nor touch him with my hands or lips. We would not sense the vibrations of our voices, nor hear our words, nor even the rhythm of our breathing.

This would not be the vampire's shadowy Gift. He would not empty me of my humanity and offer instead eternity built upon the blood of the innocent victims he killed.

The man who would enter me through that little vein on my hand would offer the Gift of light that would return me to life, the simple, beautiful life of a mortal woman.

One day, somewhere, not long ago, that man I did not know decided, without having to, to take his time and travel to some trivial place, most likely, to do the thing he had chosen to.

Maybe it was at a shopping centre.

There, they sat him down in an armchair or had him lie on a stretcher. After a few routine questions, a nurse stuck a needle into the soft part of his arm and hurt him.

When I leave this place, I'll go with that other person inside me.

INDELIBLE VIRGINIA

When she placed the tray on the low table, Nessa knocked over the opaline blue vase that was her mother Julia's favourite. It broke when it fell to the floor.

Her father roared. He fulminated. He groused. He claimed they wanted to take everything that remained of her away from him.

✢

In a defensive crouch in his armchair, he muttered to himself. An old ill-tempered bear licking his wounds, opening them up again to reawaken the pain, right there, where it always is. Under the skin, pus.

The dignified patriarch before them, parading through the salon, drinking delicate sips of tea between two complacent comments, *oh, how terrible, so utterly cruel for you, just imagine it*. And urged on, he expanded, *in life it's not the same if you only knew no one could ever face*.

A nasty character with the women of the house. An ogre. The mother, devoured. The older sister, stifled. Now it was Nessa's turn. Then probably Virginia's. If there was anything left. If the false brother didn't grab

all of it, and destroy it all. One small rape after another.

In front of the father, the women were always together,
standing very close to one another. Not taking each
other's arm or hand, but their dresses touched. Their
silence formed a wall of bricks to protect them from what
had despoiled them over these last four years.

※

In her bed, Virginia was screaming and struggling. She
scratched Leonard's face and tried to strangle him.

They moved Leonard away from her. And tied
Virginia down.

Leonard cried, *What's the matter with you, Virginia?
I've never hurt you. I've always loved you. I've always taken
care of you!*

Virginia screamed the crudest insults imaginable at
him.

He left the room, slamming the door.

In the next room, he thrust his hands into a bowl of
cool water and rinsed his injured face. He was crying.

※

Virginia was serving tea in the strictest respect of
Victorian customs. But her slip was showing and the lace
was hanging free.

Leonard bought a house far from London. Away from everything. So the beast in her would not reawaken.

Virginia was serving tea the way she'd learned at fifteen in the dark house at Hyde Park Gate. Everything seemed in perfect order. But Nessa saw how her sister's hands trembled.

⚬✕⚬

Lying by the currant bushes, Virginia stretched and laughed in the sunlight with Vita. She talked. Vita listened. She was talking about Vita being a hermaphrodite.

Suddenly, Vita got up and spoke. *You don't even have a sex. All you know about is writing and talking!*

She stalked off angrily.

⚬✕⚬

It started with a thick fog that rose and moved slowly through her head. Like mist upon the sea. Virginia watched it come near. Little by little the horizon was cut off. Her train of thought became unravelled.

Virginia lay down.

The waves were forming. Crashing. Unfurling. Beating against the inside of her skull.

She put earplugs in her ears. Covered her eyes with a black velvet band. She wished she could disappear.

Inside her, everything was flying out of control, breaking apart, scattering, winging back to her in cutting shards, turning circles.

One day. Or two. Sometimes five.

Then it passed.

Or didn't. She would enter the black water full of dead fish and rotting algae.

And wouldn't emerge for another month, half dead.

✧

The house was cool, empty, and quiet. Virginia heard Nessa, Leonard, and the others laughing in the garden.

It was her birthday.

Virginia examined her face in the foyer mirror. She was searching for her mother who had died at the age she was meant to be celebrating today.

Julia was there in her features, but also, and always, in the emptiness she'd left around Virginia, and in her, when she departed.

In the big childhood house, everything was emptied of its substance, everything died with Julia. Nothing left but stick figures. A papier mâché set. Empty shells.

✧

Virginia was making rice pudding for herself and Leonard.

Leonard was ill. Maybe even seriously.

Virginia's lips moved constantly. Day and night, she muttered prayers she didn't believe in.

The world was crumbling.

Tell Leonard how much… Hold his hand so he won't slip away.

※

It was cold. They'd run out of coal. Virginia was writing. Her fingers were frozen like the pond she looked at through the window.

Something was missing in her story. Something was always missing.

She consulted the pages again, covered with scratched out words. She added more. Corrected. Recopied. Changed.

Suddenly it happened. Like galloping horses. Images fighting to be written. She could see it all. Her mind was knotted and tense. The entire book was in her head.

Don't lose anything. It flowed from her fingertips.

Three weeks of grace. The rhythm, frenetic.

Then, inevitably, the fog. Once more.

※

No letter from Nessa this morning. Nessa hadn't written for ten days.

Virginia walked circles around herself. Accused Leonard of spending too much time in London. Neglecting the dogs.

Virginia locked herself in her room. She composed a letter to her sister.

When you're not there the colour goes out of life, as water from a sponge; and I merely exist, dry and dusty.

THE WOMAN IN THE RIVER

On this February morning, the woman went down to the beach, though she had sworn she'd never go back there during the winter. For several years now, before resuming her long walks, she would wait patiently for the ice to break up on the river in a powerful, low-pitched uproar, with constellations of broken glass and the floes drifting toward the sea, urged ahead by contrary currents.

But now she had returned, attracted by the call of open space. The call was the one she dreaded.

She took her time deciding. Her footsteps in the snow proved that much as they followed a path a little lower than the one she often took in summer and fall, alone most of the time.

First the woman walked back and forth, ten metres or so in each direction, compulsively repeating the same short trajectory. Slowly, at first. A swaying kind of walk. Her traces showed that, too. Then she went faster.

She even fell at one point. Unless she let herself go on purpose. The imprint of one of her hands, fingers outspread, was clearly visible on the hardened snow. She was wearing red woollen gloves. The fibres were found in the hollowed out spaces left by her palms and fingers.

It was twenty-eight below at dawn. In the distance, where the fast-flowing water resisted the terrible grip of the cold, the river was smoking, like a warm house in the glacial hours before dawn.

Then a single track, perpendicular to the traces of her pacing, led toward the ice. There was no hesitation in her steps. No hurry either. The traces were clean, from the heel to the tip of her toe, and well marked, like someone who knows where she is going.

At the shore and a good distance past it, great plates of ice had cracked, pushed by the slow, early winter tides, lifting, jostling, and riding upon each other in a strange ballet. The icy air caught them in their movement and created new landscapes of uprooted conglomerates of blocks rising between the smooth, shiny surfaces. But now nothing moved, even when the tides were at their highest. The wind swept the snow ceaselessly to keep the tableau clean and hard.

It looked as though the footsteps stopped abruptly where the bank ended and the river began. The woman seemed to have disappeared into the water at the very spot where she crossed the line. As if, once this limit was transgressed, a hole had opened at her feet, then closed over her, the ice lips of the river knitting together immediately.

But further on, now and again, the contour of a heel and or the imprint of part of the sole of a boot could be seen, stamped into the small accumulations of snow that succeeded, despite the northwest wind, in huddling by the protected edges of the icy mounds.

The woman had walked to the extreme limit without the frozen surface giving way.

Before her, there was nothing but a mass of black ink moving sideways, dizzying in its progress, with thick vapour rising from it. In the air was that strange, grave music of the white blocks of ice tinted with azure that the water shepherded together as it rushed forward frantically; the blocks lowed and grunted as they crashed together.

Now everything had to be thought out again. As if, standing on the bank, the woman hadn't made any decision, except to come to the edge of this liquid abyss, just to see.

Again, fear took hold of her frozen body, with all the cries held in, like a gag jammed into her mouth. The woman was paralyzed, hypnotized by the mad current flowing before her eyes, the same current that flowed under the ice that vibrated and protested beneath her feet.

She could have been discovered there, standing, covered with frost and wind-blown snow, not drowned but petrified by fear forever, never having suspected that death would come from somewhere else but the water and her desire to give herself to it.

But the woman ended up tearing herself from fear's grasp.

She knelt down and stretched out on the frozen sheet. Then she crept slowly toward the narrow border that separated *still time* from *too late*.

She slipped her body into the water, holding herself back a brief moment with her fingertips on the edge of the ice. Small traces of red wool stuck there, too.

Then, in an instant, the woman passed over to the other side of things.

❧

From a house, not far off, an old lady watched what happened, and could do nothing.

When the rescuers arrived, everything was quiet and deserted.

❧

The man couldn't imagine it. The woman travelling under water. With her wool gloves and her scarf around her neck. Irredeemably alone.

When they took him down to the beach, it was nearly noon. Sparkling with crystals, the air burned his eyes. The silence swallowed up human voices. The dazzling light would have you think that everything was clear and without mystery.

The man couldn't stop shivering, but couldn't tear himself away. He stayed on the bank, looking out over the emptiness. Defenceless, incredulous.

He couldn't help thinking that the woman was still standing in front of her easel, as she did every day for months at a time, pushing herself to paint another picture, though whatever she did, the colours would slough off all pigment, fade before her eyes as they always did, and turn livid. A cameo of absence.

⚭

The woman was travelling under water.

She thought she was going to die, strangled by the cold, her heart twisted in a vise. But she was there, her eyes wide open, aware.

As if in death, you could remain alive.

THE WAIT

The smell of cement dirtied by urine and excrement tormented her senses, and every pore of her skin, all the way to the bone.

The walls were covered with graffiti written in dried blood.

You might think the woman was sequestered in this hideout, but she was there of her own free will, though we couldn't really call it free.

She was sitting on a rickety chair, hands on her knees. She was looking through the windowpane.

She was totally absorbed by the scene outside. Her posture showed as much. Her body was not leaning against the chair back. She was sitting on the edge of the chair, very straight, though bent slightly forward. She had been there for hours.

The dress she was wearing was so threadbare you couldn't say whether it had been black or charcoal. It was cold inside the dank cell, even in the tropics.

The window was made of six squares of glass. Five of them had been whited out. The sixth was as well, but the woman, or someone before her, had scratched away the paint with her fingernail, like frost on a pane. The light came through the glass, dull and showing no details. It was daytime. The spotlights were blinding at night. The afternoon was running down on the square outside. Inexorably, the shadows stretched and lengthened.

The woman's hair was almost completely hidden under a scarf. The little bit you could see was black. She was not an old woman. Nor very young either. Or maybe so, though there was a kind of gravity in her attitude. A body hardened and harmed, even at her age.

The way she was positioned, you could not see her straight on, nor could you see her profile. More at an angle, an imperfect silhouette. The contour of her thin face was harsh and bony. Her cheeks were sunken, her cheekbones protruding, and her eyes deeply hidden in their sockets, her features concave.

She had been there forever, centuries, maybe, and had not moved. You might think she had turned to stone, and entered the realm of the mineral, or the dead. But that was not the case. She was alive, though she wished she weren't. Her breast scarcely moved when she breathed.

Slowly she grew aware of the unbearable through the scratches in the window glass. As if someone had poured cement into her mouth. She would never be able to scream again. She had gone beyond. Though she would go on speaking, the words would fall from her mouth like shards of cold lava.

She did not flinch. Her eyes were open, even at night. She would take in the world through the screen of what she had witnessed. Blind and all-seeing, having seen it all.

Her forehead was unlined. Her features were not twisted by tension. She had gone beyond terror. She would not know fear because the worst had already happened.

She was sitting, though her spirit was on its feet. Nothing would make her bend, whatever else happened, and despite appearances.

Outside, people were shouting. Vulgar, barbaric slogans cut through by screams of suffering.

Through the tumult, she made out the single lamentation of one man. Soon she heard only him. She was deaf to any other voice if his cry was not within it.

The woman looked out the window. She was simply that: a woman seeing and hearing. She stared at the wall; bullets had shattered the cement in many places. Others would soon come and write their chapter of horror.

She did not look away. She needed to see, to the end.

The crackling of bullets had not yet split the air. But there was blood everywhere. Men in their suffering were unrecognizable.

Worse than the detonations that had not sounded yet was the metallic laughter of the other side. Humans, too, apparently. She knew most of them.

The woman waited, unmoving.

Finally she heard the sound of machine guns.

After their work, the killers would go home. They would wash their hands carefully, then sit down at the table for the evening meal with their families.

Here, there would be silence.

For a long time to come.

Sooner or later, night would fall.

The woman would step outside with the other women who were waiting, like her, with neither cries nor tears, in adjacent cells.

Slowly, they would walk to the wall stained with death.

A LIVING SOUL

She tapped on her skin with her fingertips. Probing, tapping, she travelled across her entire body. It echoed like a staved-in drum. She was empty.

Behind the wall of soft flesh, she listened for a sound, the way she had been taught to, through the uprights and the crossbeams of her construction. But there was nothing. They couldn't even crucify her. The nails would find no purchase.

She paced circles in a room that was sealing tight around her. Her life was dominated by the imperious need to know. She couldn't stand the riddles anymore.

She subjected herself to endless cross-examination under a violent spotlight that burned her eyes and split her lips. But she never managed to find the question, the only true one that could have counted. She went astray in the labyrinth of her thoughts, formulating complicated questions that led only to further ones, ever more obscure, in which she bogged down. Toward the end, words began to dissolve of their own accord into meaningless prattle, and finally into lallation; only "Mama" could be identified.

Long before she sought refuge here, she walked through sweet-smelling forests and feverish cities. She lingered at length in broad gardens and museums. She partook until she was slaked. But her thirst returned soon after, every time, and more intense, like a tearing in her throat, shifting sands in her larynx. A cramp in her solar plexus.

She was thirsty but hungry, too, ever since she could remember. A void inside. To eat or drink, she would throw her head far back, set an enormous funnel in her mouth, and empty demijohns of red wine and bags of groceries full to the brim into it. Sometimes she inhaled whole animals, feathers, fur, and bones included. She was appeased, but the appeasement lasted only a few hours.

For a time, her voracity, that still tormented her, made her hope there was someone inside her, someone or something. She believed she was inhabited. When she stuffed herself, she imagined she was feeding that presence, the way she might feed a fire. And even if it were a monster, an ogre, she would have preferred such a creature to being an abandoned house, a deserted city. But her insatiability was tied to the feeling that everything that entered her would escape sooner or later, there was no alternative, since she was full of holes.

She resolved to stop being a transit station for perishable items. She would not dine at that table anymore. Even at the cost of her life.

She sought other nourishment elsewhere, more substantial. She would let someone penetrate her and be implanted within. A graft of being. Men arrived, but they all ended up leaving. The same happened with children she would have liked to keep forever as her final asylum.

She came to believe that the secret resided in the Verb, the eternal source of life, a permanent presence. She travelled from temple to temple, so that the sacred seed might be placed in the palm of her hand, and she might deposit it on her tongue. But as soon as she closed her mouth, the miniature man on the cross would be there, like at the end of her grandmother's rosary, but alive, thin, and bony, squirming, a little clot she couldn't swallow in one gulp. She ended up gnawing on the fine bones and spitting them out so as not to choke.

But now she stopped trying to absorb anything into her body. Quite the opposite: she made sure nothing foreign penetrated her. She cleaned house because hope had returned, though tenuous, because of a distant sound within her she wasn't even sure she'd heard, that might have been all in her head.

She wanted to see what it was like inside. Like in the old days, the way she did with the dolls people gave her. A few days after she got one, the doll mysteriously disappeared. The gifts stopped arriving the day her mother started finding the debris of dismembered dolls, ripped open and massacred, scattered through the house and yard.

She wanted to see inside, she couldn't help it. Split the seams, open slowly, lie down on her stomach, and feel around. But avoid all barbaric carnage. She had sounded out the possibilities and made her calculations to avoid making a mess.

She started by opening what opened easily. With both hands, she held the jaws wide open and thrust her head into her mouth, pushed past her narrow throat, and found herself at a crossroads. She couldn't see anything, but the sound inside was clearly audible. She stopped doubting her presence. Over and over she cried, "Who's there?" Her cries echoed back, deformed by distance, and she didn't know whether that was her voice coming back to her, or if it belonged to someone else who might be searching for her. The thought oppressed her so deeply she started suffocating, and had to go back outside.

For several hours, it seemed she was sleeping, or had died, stretched out full length on the floor in the middle of the room, perfectly motionless. But she was listening. At times she stopped breathing and listened for the furtive sound inside. It was as though someone was moving away, then growing nearer, perhaps just as thirsty for knowledge as she was.

She ended up slipping her fingers into every opening, exploring every breach, each discreet fold as if someone might be taking shelter there, having withdrawn under an overhang or behind a membranous screen.

Soon her feverish hands were thrusting in, exploring, palpating, pulling out into the light everything she could grasp onto.

On the white sheets with which she had covered the long wooden table, the kidneys and heart, the ovaries, some lengths of tripe and other things she could not name were lined up in orderly fashion. She was fascinated by the lapping of her hands in her humours and phlegm, and the sucking sound of organs pulled from their nests.

Soon her hands were not enough. She thrust her entire body into her abysses and gaping spaces. She travelled down her main arteries, then dove into the labyrinths of vessels, and quickly lost her way. Exhausted, she moved through the darkness, wondering out loud, "Where am I?"

She was running out of air.

She used a machete to cut a path and find her way back outside.

This time, she afforded herself no rest. She washed her hands and went back to work immediately.

Each organ was minutely dissected. Nothing was left to chance. Someone had to be there, somewhere.

When she reached the end of the autopsy, the body was everywhere, in disparate pieces.

But not a living soul.

Not even a cat from some dark alley.

Yet there was the sound of footsteps, always, in the distance, scattered inside her.

BEYOND REPROACH

Didier opened the door to his studio furnished with the bare essentials. The minimum was enough for him.

For the last year and a half, he had been coming here to recharge his batteries after returning from working abroad for months at a time.

But today, this place was no longer a refuge; it was a prison.

This time he returned much sooner than planned, and for good. The problem was his hands. He could not execute the expert, precision moves his work demanded. His hands shook, especially the right one. Not very much, but too much to perform surgery. Sometimes, one of them would jump suddenly. And his condition would not be getting better.

Didier stepped inside and closed the door with his foot. He dropped his bags on the floor. Without taking off his coat, he walked across the room and stood in front of the large map of the world hanging on the wall.

Red thumbtacks marked locations in Africa, South America, and Asia.

Over the last fifteen years, Didier replaced his map three times because too many borders had moved and some countries had changed names. He worked in two countries that had since disappeared off the map. And in others that were born from fractures, and that did not exist when he was there. He treated people exiled by violence into the countries surrounding theirs. Like in that refugee camp, supposedly temporary, that ended up taking hold in a neighbouring country, where people lived and waited, they had no idea for what, for more than twenty years.

Countries tear themselves apart, turn into cannibals, and wipe themselves out of existence. Others ride one over the other, swell up, and explode. Still others implode.

Didier travelled to those spots marked in red to graft bits of skin onto open flesh, reset and fix shattered bones, amputate limbs, pull out bullets, and extract shards of shrapnel from land mines scattered through human bodies.

He also removed tumours in the intestinal tract, lungs, and other parts; he performed many types of surgery. Along with social and political chaos, even when war and natural catastrophe devastate everything they touch, illness and accidents still occur. In those countries, too, children play and fall, stones go on obstructing kidneys, and babies sometimes refuse to leave their mother's bellies.

Didier stood in front of that world where his missions would no longer leave their mark.

He opened his arms wide, stretched them high, and grabbed the top of the map. Then he ripped it off the wall. The little nails went flying and scattered across the floor with a metallic sound.

Didier wasn't sure he'd be able to live without travelling and doing his work.

An irrepressible urge had always sent him to places where the needs were enormous and the means nearly non-existent. He had been invested with a noble mission. A drop of water in the ocean, and he knew it. No more, no less. But a drop that made a difference. He believed that.

Julianne, his ex-wife, put it another way: his case was a complex and sophisticated form of megalomania.

In countries ravaged by war or cataclysm, Didier could set himself up as a saviour, or even God. Something he didn't neglect to do at times.

Before he got involved in his life without borders, Didier was just another surgeon, and despite his efforts, nothing about him set him apart from the rest.

At home, he tried to build the perfect family. To achieve that, everyone needed to submit to any number of rules and precepts. There was the right way to speak, and hold oneself, and be together, and, above all, the need to maintain a playful attitude at all times.

Julianne liked that at the beginning. Even if his work was demanding, Didier participated actively in family life.

But soon Julianne realized that there was nothing spontaneous about Didier, and she began to see his stereotyped vision of the family unit. Not only did they have to follow an invisible model of the perfect little family, they had to convince themselves that they were better than other parents.

Didier filmed birthdays and special events, but also recorded moments in their daily life. In these videos, everything looked the same, and in the background was a constant malaise, barely camouflaged by bursts of laughter often performed for the camera, and Didier behind it.

Theirs was a cardboard universe behind which everything was going haywire. That became more obvious by the day.

To prop up the illusion of the ideal family, Didier deployed an extraordinary and constant energy. He resented Julianne, Mélina, and Benjamin enormously for being unable to play their roles correctly, and not corresponding to the idyllic image he had in his head.

After a few years, Didier was so disappointed that all he could think about was how to escape the trap that had imprisoned him. The possibility of working overseas was the perfect excuse.

When he returned from his first mission, Didier wasn't the same man. In just five months, he had succeeded in pulling himself out of the chaotic situation in which Julianne and the children remained stuck like flies to flypaper.

The change was radical.

Everything that used to interest and concern Didier now left him indifferent, or irritated him.

He often experienced utter boredom when he was with his wife and children. Rage would overwhelm him suddenly, and he couldn't always contain it.

It was clear that Didier had an unfulfilled need. At home, he couldn't get the high doses of adrenaline to boost him to the point where he liked to be. Everything seemed dull and lacking in challenge, even his work, compared to the exalting and dangerous experiences he'd had overseas.

One evening, Julianne tried to talk to him about how much he had changed. Not only was he not the least interested in his family anymore, he didn't seem to want to be part of it. Didier didn't answer. He walked out of the room.

The next time, he turned around and looked her in the eye and told her through clenched teeth, "I'm here, aren't I? I don't see what you've got to complain about! You've got everything! Isn't that enough?"

Tensions continued to mount in the house.

Mélina, Benjamin, and even Julianne increasingly felt that the floors of every room in their house were mined. Constant vigilance was called for. Didier exploded over every little thing and the children ended up in tears.

The situation became untenable. Julianne gathered up her courage and decided to bring up the subject with Didier again and, this time, take things to their logical conclusion.

She hadn't even finished her first sentence when he interrupted to inform her that he had signed a new contract for a second mission overseas, longer than the first. If he wasn't needed here, he would go elsewhere, where people wanted him.

The question was settled.

Didier left a week later.

His abrupt departure and everything that was left unsaid between them filled Julianne with such anger that she couldn't sleep for nights on end. Her jaw was clenched so tight it was painful, and her nails left marks in the palms of her cramped hands.

Mélina and Benjamin were so upset they didn't know whether they should mourn their father's departure, as they had the first time, or be happy he had disappeared, since they didn't recognize him anymore. He turned his attention to them only when he was in the mood to criticize them, or teach them some moral lesson.

Before he left the first time, they had to act like perfect little children to live up to his expectations, and they hadn't always liked doing that, but at least their father seemed to love them back then. He spent a lot of time with them and looked after their needs.

But now Didier had left them to save the lives of people far away, as his family was breaking up. He didn't seem to notice they were slipping into chaos.

When he went away the first time, Didier left empty places everywhere that let the life leach out of the house. The bed that was too big where Julianne slept. The chess set that Benjamin played sometimes, in the evening, in his room, pretending his father was there. He talked to him in a low voice. Mélina, who was only thirteen, tried to seduce one of her teachers, a man of thirty-four who had a certain resemblance to Didier.

Julianne tried to patch up the cracks, but they kept getting wider. Despite all she did, the walls of their house were growing ever more unstable. In certain spots they were cracking and falling into dust like the walls of cities under bombardment full of rubble and debris under which people no one could find or reach were dying every day.

The years went by and Didier continued to come and go.

Each time he returned, instead of noticing that his wife and children were fighting to keep their head above water, Didier considered that they were wallowing in a universe of luxury, and that their life was both abject and indecent.

Some evenings, when the four of them were seated at the table, Didier found the conversations so insipid, the problems thought to be the day's drama so insignificant, the abundance in his plate, on the table, and everywhere else so excessive that he jumped up, often abruptly, knocking over his chair. He rushed outside for a brisk walk to keep from screaming out his disgust.

Julianne and the children lost their appetite. They felt inadequate and uninteresting. They were ashamed of being healthy, and having enough to eat, and living in their beautiful big house. Ashamed of almost being happy when they were together, without Didier.

When he was there, it was automatic: they lived in a stifling atmosphere of insecurity and guilt.

He made it his business to remind them how lucky they were to be in a country where peace and abundance reigned. Overabundance, he pointed out, superfluous wealth and waste. Hatefully, he attacked their indifference and lack of awareness, their insatiability and their frantic individualism.

Didier took pleasure in telling them stories, especially over Sunday supper, about the horrors he witnessed in the countries he had visited during his missions.

He put so much emphasis and added so many realistic details that Mélina started having nightmares.

She even began refusing to eat because children were starving to death elsewhere in the world, they were sick and often orphaned, and many times suffered from all those ordeals at once.

But later, as soon as her father launched into one of his lessons or horror stories, Mélina would slip away. When Didier saw her moving for the door, he would call after her, "That's right, stay in your cute little cocoon! Your crass ignorance. Close your eyes and your ears! You're just a coward, Mélina!"

Julianne joined the fray as Benjamin took advantage of the uproar to disappear, too.

In the end, Didier stopped his moralizing lessons and stories of atrocities. He lost all hope of saving his family. In any case, Mélina and Benjamin deserted the house whenever their father wasn't overseas.

The day after Didier returned from one of his trips, Julianne announced she was filing for divorce. Didier seemed relieved. A week later, he was living in his little studio.

Julianne wanted a divorce long before then, but she had put it off because of Benjamin.

From Didier's first trip, and over the following years, Benjamin did everything in his power to win his father's love and attention. His efforts were in vain. And his last attempt was a miserable failure.

After high school, where he had an undistinguished record, Benjamin signed up for social sciences at a college. His father told him he wasn't surprised. Only losers and lazy kids chose the social sciences, especially when no math was involved.

Benjamin was deeply hurt, but instead of pitying himself, he decided to prove to his father that he was neither lazy nor a loser. He worked very hard and got excellent grades.

At the beginning of his fourth session, he knew what he wanted to do, not only for a living, but with his life. He waited eagerly for his father to return so he could tell him.

The day Didier came back, Benjamin announced he'd been accepted at the university of his choice in the department of social work. He was going to build a career working with street people.

Benjamin had pictured his father's reaction several times. First he imagined his surprise. Then, his pride.

Following his footsteps, his son would get involved in humanitarian aid.

But Didier didn't react the way Benjamin had hoped, not at all. He burst out laughing and, getting up from his chair, told Benjamin, "You need a university diploma to do that?" He left the room in a peal of self-satisfied laughter.

Benjamin didn't go to university even though he'd been accepted. He retreated to his room and for months did nothing but play video games. Then he left home and went to live with some friends.

Since the divorce, Benjamin stopped seeing his father and never spoke another word to him.

Mélina turned fifteen. She dressed completely in black and lost so much weight she put her life in danger.

For the last three months, she has been living in a special home for anorexics. Her father refuses to see her. He pointed out to her that people were actually dying of hunger because they actually had nothing to eat. Whereas she, Mélina, was playing at being sick. He would not allow her to manipulate him. He would not stand by, powerless, as she let herself die slowly but surely. He had better things to do: help people who really were dying of hunger.

Julianne is still there for Mélina and Benjamin, but that doesn't seem to be enough.

A DROWNING

Floating on the surface of the water: her goldfish. With a net, she retrieved it carefully from the aquarium. She placed it on a paper towel, not knowing what to do with it. She couldn't just throw it in the garbage, or down the toilet.

Just as she had never known what to do, over the last thirty-five years, with her dead cats, her birds, her turtles, her dwarf rabbit, and her two dogs.

She ended up burying them, all of them.

The way she'd buried the women and men in her life.

Standing by the counter, she cried silently. Her tears dropped onto the paper towel.

Ever since she was a little girl, death had put an end to every bond.

A RECURRING PATTERN

Catherine extended her hand toward her computer and touched the screen with the tip of her index finger. A little off to the right was a small circle where she saw nothing. Part of her finger and the text disappeared, swallowed by a black hole. As if someone had cut out and thrown away a teardrop of reality.

Six months ago, Catherine developed an extra blind spot in her field of vision. The small white speck on the surface of one eye was a souvenir of Pittapat, her old tiger-striped cat. There was nothing ferocious about him, but the day she placed him on the veterinarian's table for the last time because he was too sick, the cat suddenly sensed his life was in danger, and he leapt at Catherine in an attempt to escape. He had never reacted that way before. The claw to her eye put an abrupt end to sixteen years of friendship. Catherine didn't scream. She felt an intense burning pain and a thick fog passed over her. She woke up in emergency. Pittapat was dead. It was a total disaster.

She went back to writing her text.

Pittapat was not replaced and never would be. When she worked, he always perched on her desk, and he followed her everywhere. She missed him.

Before, she never felt like she lived alone. Now she had that feeling all the time, and it was more painful than a corneal lesion.

Sometimes she felt a pain in her heart, especially when she came home to her apartment where no one was waiting for her, not even an old cat. She would put on music, but that wasn't enough. The emptiness was so dense she could reach out and touch it, like a wall of ice.

She couldn't even lose herself in her work anymore.

In the morning when she woke, the prospect of living through another day overwhelmed her. She had to gather her courage just to get out of bed. Sometimes she would start to cry. She left her bedroom and gazed at the large painting with the poppies, but its magic didn't work anymore. Coffee had lost its taste and so had the pieces of bread she used to dunk into her soft-boiled egg.

Her blue suitcase sat in the hallway. Last night she brought it upstairs from her locker in the basement of the building. A trip used to serve as an escape, an anesthetic. She wasn't sure she wanted that kind of flight this time.

She kept a box of violet-flavoured candies in her desk drawer, and she slipped one into her mouth. Her work was going nowhere. She might miss her deadline. That had never happened before.

Something had broken inside her.

She got up and looked out the window at the parking lot. No one was coming to visit. She always broke off with the people she loved. And it wasn't because she didn't need anyone – on the contrary.

It was like a mistake in her technique, a recurring pattern that, ever since she was a child, had taken hold in her and kept repeating itself in the mural of her life. She would have liked to act differently, but every time she tried to change, a moment always came when she feared everything would collapse and sweep her away as it fell. Against her will, she would return to the old pattern recreated with the obsession of minutia.

She turned on the television. A documentary about mites held her attention for a moment. She learned that millions of these tiny beings shared her bed. On another channel, a leopard had just captured a deer, and was devouring it even before it was dead. Catherine switched off the set.

In the hallway, her hands against the wall, she cried silently. She went into the kitchen and drank a glass of water. She had stopped sitting at the table for her meals. She ate less and less and when she did, she gobbled her food in the living room, in front of the TV. She wished she could forget there was no one, but she couldn't.

The phone rang. Catherine quickly dried her tears on her sleeve, cleared her throat, and picked up the receiver.

Her voice betrayed none of her distress. She laughed and talked in a calm, detached tone. André was offering her another contract. Over the last two years, she'd had no worries, the money was coming in. But she'd just about stopped buying records and books the way she used to.

She hardly went out at all. Fatigue had entered her and weighed her down. Her arms and legs were heavy and everything was an effort.

After a few minutes, the conversation took a different turn. Catherine felt her body stiffen. Once again, she reminded André that she preferred to maintain a professional friendship with him.

Before, they used to enjoy having lunch together from time to time, to talk about work and other more ordinary things. Their enjoyment grew. One day, André invited Catherine over for dinner. The invitation was a threat in her eyes. They broke off their lunch dates.

She hung up and stood there, her hand on the receiver. Then she began to hit her head against the partition, gently.

When she was little, the neighbours had a Dalmatian. She used to watch it between the boards of the fence that her father made the dog's owner build. She would slip her fingers through the crack and Pichou would lick them.

Catherine's parents told her that all dogs could turn nasty. They showed her a photo in the newspaper of a little girl who had been bitten in the face by a golden retriever that was supposedly very tame. The day her father caught Catherine in the yard next door, petting Pichou, he grabbed her by the arm and dragged her back home, then hit her. Behind the fence, Pichou barked and barked, something he never did.

She didn't know why she remembered the Dalmatian now. Maybe because of the deer on TV. Or André's call.

You can't trust anyone, her mother used to say. Even Pittapat. Catherine had been naïve enough to think her cat was different. The scar on her cornea proved otherwise. She shouldn't have trusted him.

The world backed up what her parents had driven into her: without exception, other people were her enemies, and they wanted to devour her. All predators. Most of all, she had to watch out for nice people. The nasty ones were no problem, she stayed away from them anyway.

She sobbed this time as she pounded the wall with her fists. She couldn't stop. Catherine didn't hold back, even if her neighbours might hear. When she finally stopped crying, she felt completely exhausted, but the tension had left her throat. She could breathe easily, and that surprised her.

She walked to the sliding door and opened it wide. The air felt good. The late afternoon light was soft. A pigeon flew past and settled on the edge of the roof at the corner of the building. For the first time, she didn't think about the droppings. The sun turned the bird's feathers iridescent.

Catherine wanted nothing more to do with the blind spot in her life that stole a piece of reality from her – the most beautiful part.

She turned to the phone and called André back. Her voice was raspy, her tone unsure. She didn't try to hide those things.

Tomorrow, Catherine would go to his house for dinner.

HEART OF ICE

Easter. The women were walking along the snow-covered beach. Their arms were linked and they were talking in low tones. And laughing.

The two were in what people call the prime of life. They had passed several milestones. They were happy with themselves these days.

Jacques Cartier Beach, where the story first began. They were together by the water, the way they'd been as girls on the Richelieu. The water, their mother.

Normally they never went down to the beach before the snow melted, and the ice on the river broke up completely. But they wanted to see the spring tides. An astonishing landscape, both violent and tender. The waves casting blocks of ice onto the banks. Then taking them back. And returning them again.

Everywhere, at their feet, were small transparent shards of azure ice. The older woman's birthstone.

Here and there lay metre-long blocks, transparent and also shaded with blue. The light made them iridescent in places. The women ran their hands along the rounded edges. The ice melted slowly in the warmth of their palms.

They would have liked to lick the cubes the way they did when they were little, along the Richelieu, when they licked salt blocks in which the cows' tongues sculpted pretty little hollows.

But they wouldn't lick the blocks, even if they did look like barley sugar. They were adults now, and knew the river was sick under the surface.

They were big and they knew, but they didn't know everything.

They didn't know, but would find out in a few days, that one of them was sick under the surface, too. One of them was not, as they thought, in the prime of life. One of them, very soon, would enter the ice and be lost in the heart of a nameless ocean.

THE PERFUME
OF YLANG-YLANG

The first time she appeared to him, it was just before noon in the latticework of alleys in a Mediterranean city. She was walking straight toward him. Her face was pale and her ecru suit must have been linen. When he saw her, he stopped in his tracks, as if struck by a dizzying flash of light. He thought she would accost him, or maybe run right into him. But at the last moment, she turned and moved into a side alley, leaving a flower perfume that he recognized, though could not name.

He moved into that alley and watched the woman until her image faded in the distance, into the white and ochre walls and their load of light. As if she had issued from those walls, and was now returning there. He hadn't seen where she had come from; he was too busy gazing at a window from which a song of incredible sweetness flowed.

All afternoon, he walked in search of her, through the labyrinth. He had no eyes for the entryways to the houses where women and children gathered in the coolness of the shadows, nor for the red geraniums in clay pots set on the ancient paving stones, nor the small rickety chairs leaning by the doors, nor the Venetian blinds the same blue as the sky, nor the borders of the terra cotta roofs. His eyes criss-crossed the space in front of him as he scrutinized intersections and examined each direction, hesitating, then hurrying down the street he chose, nearly running.

He had decided to begin his journey here, a place he had already been, to avoid that morbid frenzy that overtook him every time he entered a foreign territory. At times like that, something grasping and nervous awoke in him, an uncontrollable appetite, a voracious hunger he could scarcely master. His solitary travels in foreign lands were the only time he lost the cool-headedness that was his trademark.

He did not do anything extraordinary during these trips. He walked, from morning to night. Quickly. In search of something, though he knew not what. Late in the evening he would return, exhausted, to his room; despite the days he stayed there, it remained totally foreign to him. But that was what he was after, that strangeness and the dissociation that put him in a state of anxiety, but with his mind completely open.

He needed to be shaken up that way, painful as it was. He prepared himself for the transition; he began most of his travels in a city he had some knowledge of, and often ended his trip by coming back for several days to the same place that acted, in a way, as his decompression chamber. The few times he did not employ this strategy, the trip was difficult and the return disturbing, as if his mind had not been able to catch up to his body.

This time, something unexpected had shaken the decompression mechanism, and he found himself lost in the depths.

The woman he had seen, and lost, had that effect on him.

When the walls grew dark and the alleyways began to fill with footsteps, voices, the rattle of cooking pots, and the smell of spices and lamb, the man emerged from the labyrinth and headed toward one of the wide squares. The outdoor cafés were packed with men, and only men, drinking, smoking, and talking loud, their arms wide open and their hands like windmills. He glanced at his watch. The routine would last another hour. Then the men would go home, and return when night settled in.

The man was hungry and thirsty. He sat down on the lip of a fountain and splashed his face. As he stood again, he cursed the thing in himself that, every year, pushed him to leave for two months and immerse himself in worlds where he was fated to be an outsider, a man excluded, a foreign body.

But he needed that panic and the distance that made everything seem different, even him, even his life. When he was in the trance of travel, death itself lost the power to terrify. During his many trips, he had had three brushes with death. He was shaken, yes, but in an unexpected way. As if death had been one more experience, a deeper kind of travel. Another place to explore.

He didn't eat much that evening, but he drank a lot. He lost his way going home. Old women were sitting outside in the cool of the evening, but he didn't ask anyone for help. Dogs were drinking water from a gutter in one of the streets. Children were rolling metal hoops down the uneven cobblestones. Women were folding sheets in half, and shaking them out vigourously. He preferred to stay lost and walk forever, despite being tired, than speak to another human being.

Except at the hotel and other places where he had no choice, his travels were carried out in complete silence most of the time. He didn't want to hear or use a language in which he might recognize himself.

He ended up finding his hotel and he went up to his room. He sat down on the unmade bed and cried. That hardly ever happened to him. He lay down without getting undressed and fell asleep.

Voices in the next room woke him at dawn. A couple was quarrelling. A door slammed. The man went to the window. A woman dressed in black was leaving the hotel. Once, in a village in the middle of the country, he saw a woman being stoned. His whole body trembled as he watched, and his hands grasped at his face and his head shook. The execution didn't take much time. Once the square emptied out, he went to the woman who had been left for dead and saw she was still breathing. The cuffs of his pants were stained with blood. He hurried away as if he were guilty of her murder, and left the village as fast as he could.

He lingered at the window a while. Day was breaking through a light mist that cast a lavender hue on the walls of the houses.

He took a shower and dressed, then went out. The café he chose wasn't open but it wouldn't be long; the waiters were busy inside. He stood in the middle of the quiet little street.

Then he heard the sound of high heels slowly beating the stones of a nearby street. The footsteps drew closer.

The woman he was looking for the day before appeared. She turned in his direction and moved toward him. She wasn't a woman of this country, but she belonged to these walls and this light.

She swept past him, very close, and went into the café that had just opened. He closed his eyes and thought of the flower whose perfume, in another place and time, had once touched him so deeply. But the name escaped him.

In the café, he chose a table from which he could watch her. She was sitting near a double window that opened onto a tiny garden.

When she left, he followed her at a discreet distance. It didn't take long before he lost her. All that day, he walked in vain.

This morning, at dawn, he returned to the same café. She wasn't there. He sat at one of the tables overlooking the garden.

He didn't have to wait long. She came and sat down.

She looked outside, her hands clasped on the white tablecloth.

They sat that way until the waiter brought their coffee. He hardly dared look at her.

Then she began speaking to him in a foreign language he did not recognize, and that probably didn't exist, or if it did, it hadn't been discovered. She spoke slowly. Her eyes were like the nearby sea. She leaned across the table, speaking low, gently, at length. It was as if she were singing. He could see the tops of her breasts and felt their warmth.

Then she went quiet, lowered her eyes, and touched the man's hand on the table.

Then it was his turn to speak. He didn't try to find out whether she knew the language he used. His voice was broken, as if he were about to cry. She listened to every word, with the same intensity he had when he listened to her.

Later, when the customers started coming in for lunch, she stood up and bent low to give him a soft kiss on the mouth. Then she went outside.

At that moment, when she bent slowly over him, and the jacket of her ecru suit opened gracefully over her naked breasts and dark nipples, he remembered that little island, part of the Indonesian archipelago, Sula, it was called, and not only did he discover the heady perfume of the ylang-ylang flower, but he recalled where he had seen her, a fleeting vision that had struck him dumb for a moment in his wild headlong rush, like a premonitory dream quickly forgotten.

He followed her out of the café and through the labyrinth of alleys where he had spotted her the first day. They walked for a long time as if, between the two of them, there was still much distance to cover.

She led him into a cool, dim corridor that opened onto a tiny inner courtyard full of greenery and flowers. They made love slowly, standing, against the wall bathed in sunlight. She spoke to him in a low voice, not stopping for breath, and her words entered him like an enchantment.

He never saw her again, and he did not need to search for her anymore.

He went on his way, but without haste now.

In every city he travelled to, she would write to him. He would recognize her perfume on the paper. And the accents of her language that, little by little, he would recognize as his own.

When the man returned home, she would be inside him.

SAPPING

With his tongue, Gaël tried in vain to catch the chocolate ice cream running down his hand. If it dripped onto his overalls, his mother would bawl him out for sure, maybe even hit him.

The afternoon heat gathered in the asphalt of the parking lot. His mother made him sit at the edge, on the concrete border, to eat his ice cream cone.

When she was pregnant, the woman dreamed of a child who would look more like a doll than the little boy who always wanted to run off somewhere. So she wouldn't have to track him down, she kept him on a leash she tied to the clothesline in the backyard, or to the service tree in the front.

The boy was completely absorbed in licking his ice cream cone without making a mess.

He didn't see his father's jeep at the corner. He didn't hear the sound of acceleration. He scarcely noticed the squealing tires and the metallic protests as the vehicle turned and pulled into the parking space next to where he was sitting.

The sudden encroachment of the red mass in his field of vision made him look up in surprise.

His ice cream fell onto his clothes and landed on the ground.

The jeep came to a stop inches from his gym shoes.

His father jumped out. His voice was mocking as he moved toward the house, calling out to Gaël.

"Got you again, eh, kid? You have to keep your eyes open!"

THE WOMAN IN THE ALLEY

A shot of caustic acid ran through his brain.

It never lasted long. No longer than rumblings of an earthquake. But always damage, a little more each time.

He experienced something similar at the beginning. As soon as he dozed off, nightmares erupted behind his eyelids.

With time, he built a defence against them, and slept nearly three months without the debris of horror sticking to his retina when he awoke.

Then it came back. By day and by night. When he was awake. He wasn't struck by the horror – it was something much worse.

The man leaned against the concrete wall. He was soaked with sweat. He tried to recover his sense of self. The air was burning, heavy with dust and nauseating smells. He wiped his face with his shirttail.

He was alone in the alley, except for the woman he had killed and a dead dog.

He didn't look at either, but he smelled the putrid stink of one and the metallic odour and the oversweet blood of the other that mixed in with the clotted brains seeping from her right eye socket. The viscous matter had splattered back in his face, and he had vomited on the spot.

The man had never done that before: aimed for the eye.

He wasn't a real killer, that's what he always told himself, even though, over the last year and a half, he'd killed eight people and missed a few more.

He never chose his targets. He received instructions.

Like for the woman lying next to him. He'd had to track her for over three weeks to get a bead on her. Usually, she had a bodyguard.

A secret encounter sent her out on her own despite the danger, and she went walking, disguised as an anonymous citizen, down the alley of this unrecognizable city with its high-tension atmosphere.

When the bullet burst her skull open, the grey wig she was wearing lifted from her head and fell sideways across her face as she crumpled to the ground.

He hid in exactly the right spot to step out in front of her and take aim.

The first time he waited for her, he hadn't chosen his place well. And he didn't recognize her right away. She was wearing the same wig, now thick with blood, and the same makeup that made her look older, with the same threadbare clothes and black lace-up shoes.

He recognized her too late; her hand that swung with each step and brushed her dress gave her away. He knew it was her when he saw the smooth white skin of her hand, her long thin fingers, and her perfect nails that she had stripped of polish and left bare for the occasion.

He liked it better when he was given a man as a target.

He loved women in a way he considered infantile and naïve. It was absurd.

He couldn't help believing that all women held something sacred in them, naturally, though it might be solidly locked away in the unreachable depths of their being. Even the most vile and inhuman among them, like the one on the ground by his feet, almost touching him.

It was because of his mother, though there was nothing exceptional or exemplary about her, at least not that you could see. But when he was very young, he felt the presence of her luminous heart that was greater than her completely mediocre life. The presence of a kind of beauty that transcended her, whatever awkward and miserable things she did in her everyday life, with him and other people, when she was at the end of her rope. And she often was.

Two years earlier, as the minutes ticked by and his mother lay dying in his arms, as they watched each other intently, he witnessed her sacred part leave its hiding place and migrate slowly to her face. At the moment of death, she was illuminated by that sacred thing whose existence he felt early on, and had dearly loved.

She had been wounded by a bullet in a demonstration, and friends had managed to carry her, with great difficulty, through the retreating crowd, to his house. It was the end. She had lost a lot of blood, but was still able to give him this final offering: the sacred part visible in her eyes and on her skin.

He wasn't leaving the alley, though he should have, while he still could.

He leaned over the woman and uncovered her face. A pinkish jelly was smeared over it as if someone had applied a thick beauty mask. A thin veil covered her undamaged eye that had stayed open.

There was nothing of what he feared in her face or eyes.

He felt enormous relief.

He would keep this as his final image of the woman, and not the other one that had imprinted itself on his mind as he stepped out in front of her, and she saw him.

He finally left the alley.

When he got home, he undressed and showered. He rubbed his skin hard and the water was much too hot.

He came out of the bathroom and walked to the refrigerator. He took a beer and popped it open with his finger, then drank it down in a couple of gulps.

Images flooded through his mind. Banks of eyes followed him. Sometimes they caught him, captured him, a leech refusing to let go. They appeared and disappeared, piling up one over the other until they blocked out everything and blinded him.

They formed a black screen, and on it was the look the woman in the alley gave him. The man struggled for air. His legs were weak. He slipped to the floor, a ragdoll.

It took him a minute to recover. He pulled himself up to the standing position, got another beer, and collapsed into the armchair.

A little later, he went back to the bathroom and threw his shirt into the sink to soak it. It smelled like dead dog.

With his fingernail, he scraped off the sticky flecks of brain. They would go down the drain and into the sewers, and disappear like all those kids who were daring enough to challenge the system, including his younger brother. He was among the ones shot and thrown into the sewage canal on the south end of the city.

Usually he never wore a good shirt when he had a mission, but this time the target was more important than the others.

The woman was the Minister of Order and Security's wife. She was beautiful and haughty, and with her long skillful fingers, she cleverly manipulated the levers of power by using her husband. Certain that the more horrible decisions concerning the fate of the protestors carried her signature. Blood red, like the colour of her perfect fingernails and full lips.

He had dressed carefully because he didn't want that cruel, arrogant woman to take him for an ordinary small-time criminal who was using the explosive political situation to exercise his personal violence.

The woman was walking down the alley on her way to a secret encounter.

That piece of information shook the simplistic idea he had of her.

So there was a secret lover, and she was putting her life in danger for him. That possibility was something new.

Behind the pitiless official image, was there another more vulnerable woman?

That was the woman he encountered back in the alley.

In her eyes, just before he shot her, that's what he had seen: her desolation as she realized that the love between her and the man she was going to see was over. Their private love affair that was outside history.

He hesitated an instant before pulling the trigger, but she had seen his face and, if they arrested him, he wasn't sure he'd be able to keep quiet when they tortured him.

So he fired. He aimed for her eye.

He couldn't explain that.

During his training, he had been advised, as much as possible, to avoid any eye contact.

Because of his inexperience and, later, in other circumstances, he had made eye contact with seven of his fourteen targets, whether he had hit them or not.

For a fraction of a second, each of his targets had turned into a human being.

The first times, they entered his flesh like lightning bolts that kept pushing to the surface when he least expected it.

He swore he would avoid his targets' eyes.

But instead, he started seeking them out. Never, not even once, had their eyes revealed anything but the human.

In the eyes of the woman in the alley, the sacred had emerged. Just before he fired.

THE ULTIMATE

It's not like anything else.

Right away you look for words that might name it, even from a distance, as a kind of reassurance. A pile of rubble. Ruins. A heap of debris containing shattered rocks, shreds of clothing, and shards of glass. Maybe flesh, too. The ferrous bitterness of fresh blood in the air, the smell of raw organs, the slaughterhouse – all things too intense not to return to.

But it's more than that. There wasn't bombing, or an explosion or cataclysm. It wasn't a mass grave where bodies were mixed into the rocky ground with the help of a bull-dozer to hide proof of the massacre.

And it wasn't as if we had arrived afterward, too late, after everything had happened. We wouldn't have known what we were supposed to do there, only that we were at the heart of something.

Last night, we fell asleep peacefully, believing this morning would be like all the others, with the trail of sunlight on the table and on our hands, the taste of coffee and bread on our tongues. But the normal passage from night to dawn did not occur.

Suddenly it was noon. We woke up standing, our eyes wide open, here on this vast arid plain. We closed our eyes to awaken fully. Then opened them again. It was no dream. Only this in front of us: these ruins of nothingness, and an endless view stretching on forever, without buildings, without trees, without animals, without people.

Maybe we should have fled right away, it wouldn't have mattered where because it was all the same, run full speed toward the horizon. But there was this irrepressible need to put words on it before we ran for safety, and maybe understand, even a little, before we turned away.

Now there is no more escape, we know it, and it isn't a bad thing. There's nothing left but to give in to the attraction. Now we have grasped the dark force that has drawn us from the very beginning, sucking us in and leading us slowly toward chaos, and soon, it's clear, nothing of ourselves will be identifiable again.

Despite appearances, we won't be victims, not the way others might think, that we were subjected to brutal aggression, ground into dust, annihilated.

It was just an extreme experiment – the ultimate, perhaps – vaster and more mobile than language, and we agreed to experience it to the very end.

Just to see. The way we always wanted to see the rest, before, even if it meant, sometimes, not returning.

THE SPINNERS
(WHAT CAME NEXT)

The three sisters took out the skeins of wool with their rich and varied colours, the wooden frame, the distaff, and the scissors they had thrown into the dungeon of forgetfulness a long time ago.

They had decided to stop spinning the silky thread of life, which was their gift to men. They stopped spooling it across fields of time, then cutting it off, when the hour was right, to preserve the harmony of the world.

And so they had given up their patient and secret woman's work that creates life and accompanies it to the very end.

Outside, the madness of men, already so great, had gone beyond all limits in its fanaticism, cupidity, barbarity, and indifference.

Nothing could appease their greedy gaze.

And nothing touched them with its grace, even if Elpis, the youngest of the women who had sought refuge among the Spinners, told them that, down below, most human beings resisted as best they could the madness of the pitiless, all-powerful minority. Those humans needed the women to believe that their resistance was not in vain.

Even if the three sisters had lost all hope, they agreed to transmit the art of spinning fragile human lives to the younger women.